So that night, Jack just pretended to close his eyes, and when everyone in the house was fast asleep, Jack took a sack to put his dreams in and a clean white handkerchief to blow his nose with.

Then he crawled ...

down,

down,

down,

Jack and the Dreamsack

Laurence Anholt
illustrated by Ross Collins

BLOOMSBURY
CHILDREN'S
BOOKS

"The trouble with dreams," said Jack, "is that you are always asleep when you have them.

Tonight I will stay awake when I go to sleep. Then I will be able to see my dreams properly – I might even catch some and bring them home with me."

to the deep, delightful Dreamtime to search for the middle,
the very centre of all dreams everywhere.

He hadn't gone far when he found –

pink twins in pink beds,

a baby with a pram,

a small white snail dog,

a horse pulled by a man.

"Now that," said Jack, "is AMAZING!"

He crawled through a wild and dangerous Bookmaze where long words lurked in the leaves, and on the way, Jack filled the sack with a hundred things you've never dreamed of.

He collected ...

a nest full of pig's eggs,

a mouse with wooden hair,

telephones with beards,

trousers for a chair.

"Well that," said Jack, "is AMAZING!"
And the Dreamsack grew big and round.

On and on into the Dreamtime, towards the place
that is the middle, the very centre,
the very belly button of all dreams everywhere,
Jack dragged the heavy sack.

Through the Finger Forest where
the branches snap and clap.
A broken rainbow made him sad,
a leaping river made him glad,

through the Human Zoo without a ticket.

He saw unlikely cars,

incredible beds,

uncomfortable chairs,

and he rode on impossible bikes.

"There's no doubt about it," said Jack, "this really is AMAZING!"

All through the wonderful night Jack wandered,
dreamcollecting, until at last he came to the
giant Fruit Salad tree that grows right in the middle,
smack-bang in the centre, in the very belly button
of all dreams everywhere.

And Jack began to climb ...

up,

and
up,

and up.

On the very top leaf of the very top twig of the very top branch of the giant Fruit Salad tree that grows right in the centre, smack-dab in the middle, in the very belly button of all dreams, Jack found a tiny Dreamseed and wrapped it carefully in his clean white handkerchief.

As morning rose, the sack was full, and Jack suddenly thought of HOME.
So he hauled and heaved and dragged that sack, because dreams are heavy things ...

back,

and back,

and back,

to the Hohum Humdrum Waking World where he tipped the sack on his bed.

But where had the wonderful Dreamthings gone? Everything had melted away ...
A little tear rolled down Jack's cheek, "That's the trouble with dreams," he sighed.

He took out his handkerchief to wipe his eye and suddenly something shifted, and suddenly something stirred and suddenly something tumbled out – the tiny Dreamseed which immediately began to GROW ...

up,

and up,

and up.

Running to the garden just in time, Jack watched a Dreamtree grow.

Then people came from far and wide to shake Jack by the hand. He gave out slices of dreams in paper bags to the Hohum Humdrum Waking World. And it's perfectly true that new dreams grew …

day,

after day

after day.

The best kind of dreams are the wide-awake dreams,
"And those," said Jack, "are AMAZING!"